THE XTREME WORLD OF BILLY KOOL

by Phil Kettle

book:01
all or nothing

RISING STARS

CONTENTS

FILMING EQUIPMENT

Clapperboard

The clapperboard is used to mark the number and take of the scene. It helps the editor synchronise images and sound.

Gunshot Microphone

If the actors aren't wired for sound, a gunshot microphone is held above them out of camera-shot to record sound.

Boom

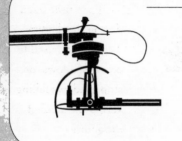

The boom is a light-weight pole, like a long arm, that holds the microphone close to the actor, but where it can't be seen.

Dolly

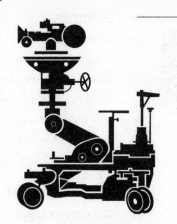

A dolly is a mobile platform that is used to mount large cameras. The dollies have all sorts of extendable arms that allow the camera to move into any position.

Studio Lights

Studio lights are used when you are filming in a studio. They are used even during the daytime. They can be used to create shadows, or stop shadows falling across the faces of the actors.

WHO ARE WE!

Hi! I'm Billy Kool and I'm the person telling you these stories. Yes! That's me. Billy Kool!

I'm not much different to most kids. Most kids think they're sports legends. I certainly do! Sometimes I imagine being a champion at every single sport that has ever been created. But I'm not. Although, last week, I really was a champion — even if it was only for a few hours.

Our school basketball team had

made it to the district final.
A reporter from the newspaper
was there so it was pretty big news.
Somehow I had the basketball in
my hands when the time clock was
running down.

Someone yelled, 'Throw the ball!'

I threw the ball from the middle
of the court. The bell sounded as it
travelled through the air. The ball
hit the hoop, rolled around and
dropped in. We won the game and
we won the championship. The team
carried me off the court!

But being a hero didn't last
very long. A week later, nobody
remembered the game at all.
I thought that the newspaper

reporter might have taken a photo of the winning shot. I went to the newsagent to check out the local paper. I walked right past the extreme sports magazine that I read every month — *Totally Xtreme* — and headed for the newspapers. I flicked through to the sports section. There was the story right at the back. My name and picture were nowhere to be seen.

I flicked through *Totally Xtreme* instead. The magazine was having a competition. They were looking for hosts for a new TV show about extreme sports.

Xtremely awesome
Xtremely cool

Have you ever wanted to be a TV star? Have you ever wanted to jump out of a plane, whitewater raft, snowboard or bungy jump? If you think you can keep your lunch down, tell us, in 100 words or less, why we should make you—and two of your best friends—the star of your own extreme sports reality TV show.

Entries close February 8th.

I told the owner of the newsagent that I was going to enter. He looked at me and said, 'You'll be lucky if they even read your entry.'

I thought there had to be more than luck if I was going to win. The letter I wrote had to be the best. After a while, I decided the best thing was just to tell the truth.

My name is Billy Kool.

I reckon that I would be a great host of a television show about extreme sports. Firstly I reckon that the show could be called **The Xtreme World of Billy Kool.** That's so the best name ever for a television show.

I also reckon that I deserve to win, because it has always been my dream to be an extreme sports star. I have two best friends who would also be really good at extreme sports. Their names are Nathan and Sally.

I also love your magazine. And I promise to keep buying it.

Thank u

Billy Kool

One of the older kids at school heard that I'd entered. 'You'll never win it, Billy Unkool.' He laughed at his own stupid joke. 'Why would they take a little nerd like you?'

If I won, my co-hosts would be my best friends, Nathan and Sally.

Nathan and I have been friends ever since I can remember. We've always played in the same football and cricket teams.

Nathan lives with his mum four houses down the road. Nathan's dad lives in another city. We never talk about his father much. Nathan just says that his dad got married again and that his life is really busy and that maybe one day his dad will have some time to spend with him.

Nathan, Sally and I still meet at our tree house like we always have. The only difference now is that we don't tell anybody. It wouldn't be too cool to admit that we still have a tree house.

Nathan has a sister who is two years older than him and she's totally cool. Her name is Crystal. I've tried to talk to her a few times, but either her hearing isn't very good or she thinks I'm a nerd. Most of the older kids at school do.

Maybe when I'm hosting my own TV show, Crystal might want to talk to me. I hope so.

Sally came to live in our street four years ago. She came from somewhere in Asia. At least, that's what we thought until she told us that she was born in the same hospital as us. Her mum and dad were born in China.

We first met Sally one day when we were playing ball in the park near our houses. Nathan had hit a high ball. I turned around to watch it fly through the air. Sally happened to be standing near where the ball was coming down.

'Catch the ball,' I yelled.

Sally caught the ball in one hand then threw it back to Nathan.

'Good catch,' Nathan said.

She just smiled like she already
knew it was a good catch.

'I'm Billy and this is my best mate
Nathan.'

'My name is Sally Wong,' she said.

Trying to be a hero, I said, 'Two
Wongs don't make a right.'

'Yeah, but one Wong could beat
one Billy any day,' she said.

That's how Sally became our
friend.

After I sent off my entry I had to
wait two whole weeks before a letter
arrived in the post.

Dear Billy

You and Nathan and Sally have been selected as finalists. We thought your letter was very original and we would like you to come to the studio for an audition on March 3rd at 4 p.m.

The competition is extreme! Five groups will be auditioned, but only one can win. Please keep in mind that we will be filming your audition, and that it will be aired on the first show, regardless of whether or not you win. Wear comfortable clothes and trainers.

Good luck
Channel Z

THE AUDITION

On March 3rd, Dad took us to the studio. Nathan was really quiet in the car. He reckoned that as soon as they saw us they would just say, 'Thanks, but no thanks.'

It looked like Sally was sitting on her hands to stop them shaking. I looked at my hands. They were still. I was cool. I was Billy Kool. I told Nathan and Sally to leave the talking to me. I had a plan. We got out of the car.

The receptionist asked us to sit in a waiting room. 'We'll call you when it's your turn,' he said.

The waiting room was full of other kids who had come to audition and their mothers and fathers.

Dad said that we were on our own and that he would wait for us in the car. Some of the kids were from school. Most of them think they're pretty good.

'Look at them—they're all wearing shades. They think they're movie stars,' Nathan said.

'They're looking at us like they think they're a lot cooler than we are,' Sally said.

'As if it's cool to sit here while your

mum does your hair,' said Nathan.

'Well, I reckon that we're as good as any of them,' I said.

A woman came into the room. 'Hi. My name is Shey. I'm the safety co-ordinator for the extreme series. I bet your parents will be pleased to hear that. My job is to make sure that you survive, and to do that you must listen and do everything that I tell you. Extreme sports aren't called extreme for nothing. If they're not done properly with all the safety precautions in place, they can be very dangerous. Extreme sports test your courage and strength, both physical and mental. Doing extreme sports pushes your body and mind

to their limits. To the very edge.
There are seven sports that we'll
be tackling in the first season of the
show. Whitewater rafting, bungy
jumping, snowboarding, skydiving,
mountain biking, kart racing and
rock climbing. If you're the lucky
ones who get to host the show, we
want you to have a lot of fun, but
remember that safety must come
first. Now, you'll all be wondering
why we asked you to wear comfy
clothes. As part of the audition you'll
be abseiling down the outside wall
of the studio—five storeys high.'

Everyone started looking around
at each other and whispering. A
couple of kids looked really pale.

I checked out Nathan and Sally quickly—they both looked normal.

'This will give us some idea about how you'll handle the different extreme sports. We're almost ready for the auditions,' Shey said. 'You'll be going through one group at a time. Good luck.'

All the other groups were called first. The mothers and fathers went with them. We were last.

'Billy Kool, Nathan and Sally,' said a voice over the PA.

A man called Lou directed us to a lift. We caught the lift to the fifth floor, then walked up a small staircase that led out onto the roof.

Lou opened the door leading onto

the roof and we walked straight out in front of two cameras.

Shey was waiting for us. 'Hi, Billy, Nathan, Sally. How are you all feeling?' she asked.

'Pretty good,' I said. I didn't think it was the right moment to mention my fear of heights. Nathan smiled at the camera. I think Sally could tell how I was feeling because she whispered, 'Imagine it will be like climbing out of the tree house.'

An abseil was set up on the roof.

'It's completely safe,' Shey said. 'The rope, the descender—which is what the rope feeds through— and your harness webbing have a breaking strain of 3000 kg. The karabiner which locks the descender to your harness has a breaking strain of 2000 kg, and the anchor is as solid as a rock. You'll control the rope with your right hand. There are two rules when you abseil. First, the thumb-in-bum rule.'

We all laughed.

'That means that you hold the rope behind your buttock. This gives you the best braking power and is safest. Second, never, ever take your right hand off the rope. There'll be a separate safety line attached so we can stop you if something goes wrong. There'll also be someone at the bottom of the abseil holding the other end of the rope — they can also stop you. Any questions?'

'Um,' Sally said. ' What do we actually do?'

Shey laughed. 'Go over the edge of the roof and lower yourself down. Sound easy?'

We put on harnesses and Shey double and triple checked them. Then she threaded the rope through the descender and locked it to my harness with the karabiner. She handed me a helmet which I put on, and then some gardening gloves. My mum would have totally understood those—the producer should make an extreme gardening show just for her. The gardening gloves were to stop rope burn as I fed the rope through.

'You're up first, Billy Kool,' Shey said. 'Don't look down.'

'Is there anything you want to say to the camera first, Billy?' the man behind the camera asked.

I racked my brains. 'I'm Billy Kool.' I looked straight at the camera. 'And I really hope I make it to the bottom.'

Everyone laughed. I hoped they couldn't hear how loud my heart was beating. I took a deep breath, walked to the edge of the roof and pulled the rope really tight. Then I stepped back over the edge.

'Go, Billy,' I heard Sally call.

At first, I barely moved because I was holding on so tight that the

rope wasn't feeding through. After
a while though, I became a lot
smoother. I even bounced away
from the wall a couple of times.
Before I knew it, I'd hit the ground.
There was a small crowd waiting for
me. Lou was there. He told me that
he was the first assistant director.
He introduced me to a woman called
Roberta.

'Well done, Billy!' Roberta said.
'You were a natural.'

Nathan came down next.

'That was awesome,' he said. He
leaned close and whispered, 'How
do you think we're going?'

'No idea,' I said.

Sally came last. When she was

about halfway down the wall, the
wind picked up and the rope started
blowing across the wall, taking Sally
with it. The person who was holding
the other end of the rope pulled tight
and Sally stopped moving. She was
stuck.

'Are you alright, Sally?' Shey
leaned over the edge.

'Yeah, I think so,' Sally said.

She had to wait there for a few
minutes. Then the wind stopped
blowing and Sally came down.

Roberta asked her if she had been
scared.

'Not really,' Sally said.

Roberta looked impressed. She
said goodbye and walked away.

After we'd all taken our harnesses off, Lou directed us back into the studio. He pointed to a door that had 'Producer' written on it, and we went in.

Roberta was sitting behind the desk. I looked at her and said, 'My name is Billy Kool. I'm Kool by name and cool by nature. I think the television show should be called *The Xtreme World of Billy Kool*. I know that my friends and I are the right people to host the show and we really want the job.'

Roberta just looked at us for a moment. Finally, she said, 'I like your style, I like your name and I think that it's great that I don't have to listen to some parent telling me how great their child is. You were all pretty brave on the wall. You've got the job.'

We smiled when she shook our hands, and said thanks. It's not that cool to show how excited you really are. We waited till we were outside, then we jumped up and down and gave each other high fives.

THE REACTION

After that, instead of being called a little nerd by older and bigger students, I was called a lucky little nerd. Nathan and Sally and I were living a dream that most people our age only read about or, of course, watch on television.

Mum and Dad told me that there had to be some rules if I was going to be part of a television show. My school work had to improve. My chores at home still had to be done.

And, most important, if I ever got a big head then I wouldn't be allowed to do the show anymore. Mum said that they needed to be sure that everything we did was safe.

I kept telling myself that everything was going to be okay. Of course it was going to be safe. Man, how would it be if I was splattered all over something on national television? There was no way that they were going to let that happen. I kept telling Nathan and Sally that the show was going to be unreal and how much I was looking forward to it. I didn't tell them about all the butterflies that were trying to escape out of my stomach.

CAST AND
CREW MEETING

On Friday afternoon, Nathan, Sally and I were waiting in my living room. Someone from the TV station was on their way to pick us up. We were going to a cast and crew meeting before our first rehearsal. Nathan said it would be like the rehearsal for the school play, where our drama teacher made us pretend to be trees.

'As if,' Sally said.

Sally couldn't wait to get to the

studio. 'It's going to be so much fun having make-up put on,' she said.

'Yeah, right!' Nathan said.

'As if Nathan and I are going to wear make-up,' I said.

Sally just grinned.

'I'm really looking forward to checking out the canteen,' Nathan said, licking his lips.

'I just want to talk to Shey about the safety equipment,' I said.

Mum told us that the car had arrived to take us to the studio. We all ran to the window.

'It's one of those really long cars,' said Sally.

'Like all the stars are driven around in,' Nathan said.

Mum tried to kiss me goodbye, but I managed to escape. How cool is it that the getaway car was a limo?

We didn't really know what to do at the cast and crew meeting so we just sat down and shut up. There were pictures on the wall with the different extreme sports on them.

'Alright, everyone,' Roberta said, 'thanks for coming. Billy, Sally and Nathan, I want to introduce you to everyone here. I met you at the audition. My name is Roberta and I'm the producer of The Xtreme World of Billy Kool.'

We all said hello. It was so weird to hear my name, Billy Kool, in the title of the show.

Roberta kept speaking. 'To my right is the director, Andrew. There are a lot of other people that we need to introduce you to, but you'll find out more about everyone who makes a TV show when you read your scripts. The first episode of *The Xtreme World of Billy Kool* will be about the audition and the making of a TV show. Then next episode, we'll start the first extreme sport — whitewater rafting. After that is bungy jumping, snowboarding, skydiving, mountain biking and kart racing. The last sport is rock climbing.'

The director took over. 'We're shooting in sequence,' he said.

'There will be two to four weeks between shooting each show, as long as it snows early in the season for the snowboarding episode. We'll have a read-through tonight and a rehearsal first thing tomorrow morning. I'll need everyone back here at 8 a.m. sharp. Ready, Billy, Sally and Nathan? Let's get started.'

I opened the script. It was really long. There was no way I was going to remember all my lines when we did it for real. I stumbled over a few words and felt my face turning red.

The next day we went back and did it for real. Nathan and I did have to wear make-up. We couldn't believe it. Sally just laughed.

MEET THE CREW

1. Roberta (Producer)

2. Joe (Camera Operator)

3. Phil (Scriptwriter)

4. Ally (Editor)

5. Lou (First Assistant Director)

6. Andrew (Director)

7. Shey (Safety Co-ordinator)

LIGHTS,
CAMERA, ACTION

BILLY
Welcome to *The Xtreme World of Billy Kool.* My name is Billy Kool and standing next to me are my co-hosts. On my left is Nathan.

NATHAN
Hi, it's great to be here.

BILLY
And on my right is Sally.

SALLY
Hi, everyone. I'm so excited that we won the audition to host this awesome show.

BILLY
This is the first of what we hope will be many shows. In the next

episode we'll be starting the extreme sports. Check us out whitewater rafting. But in today's show, you're going to meet the people who make a television show and see how a TV show gets made. You'll also get to see us auditioning.

Here, footage of BILLY, NATHAN and SALLY is inserted so the viewers can see them abseiling during their audition. The camera has a close-up of Sally's face when she is blown across the wall.

NATHAN
Of course the most important people are the stars of the show!

BILLY
Yes, the most important
people are definitely the
stars of the show.

SALLY
And that's us!

BILLY
Some of us are more
important than others.

SALLY
Yeah right. I'm the most
important.

NATHAN
How's that, Sally?

SALLY
Because you've both told
me that I have to go first
in all the extreme sports.

BILLY
Well, you didn't go first
when we abseiled.

SALLY
Yeah, but you didn't get
blown across the wall like
I did.

BILLY
We'll talk about it later.
Now it's time to meet the
team. The first person
we're going to meet is the
producer, Roberta.

ROBERTA waves.

BILLY
The producer is like
the coach of a football
team. Roberta organises
everything that happens
involving the production
of the television show.

NATHAN

Yeah, she is the boss of the show. She's like the teachers at school. What she says goes!

Here, footage is inserted that shows a planning meeting for the show that happened long before Billy, Sally and Nathan auditioned. In the footage, Roberta talks about what sort of hosts she thinks will be good for the show.

BILLY

The next most important person is the director, Andrew.

NATHAN

He plans all the shows and

he tells us what to do.

SALLY
He's the main voice that
we hear in our earpieces.
Sometimes he gets really
grumpy when we don't do
what he wants.

NATHAN
Yeah, and he gets really
grumpy when we forget what
we are supposed to say.
Andrew's main assistant
is the first assistant
director, Lou.

BILLY
And of course we
have Phil. He's the
scriptwriter. He writes
what we have to say in
each of the shows.

SALLY
Phil has the wildest-
looking hair that I've
ever seen.

NATHAN
Do you think his hair is
a wig?

BILLY
No, I think if it was a
wig he would have got one
that looks a lot better
than that.

NATHAN
Then there's Joe, the
head of the camera crew.
He shoots what you see on
your screen. When we're in
the studio, his camera is
mounted on a dolly, so the
footage will be smooth.

JOE moves from behind the camera to in front of it and waves.

BILLY
And wouldn't the show be really boring if we didn't get to hear Sally scream when she's bungy jumping.

SALLY
I know who'll be screaming and it won't be me.

NATHAN
To make sure that we can hear Sally screaming, we need a sound recordist. This is Benny.

BENNY is holding the boom above Nathan's head. A microphone is attached to the boom. Benny waves.

42

SALLY
When you're making a
television show, sometimes
you have to shoot a lot
more footage than you
actually need. So you have
to edit the tape. That
requires an editor.

NATHAN
So who is the editor?

BILLY
The editor's name is Ally.
We don't see her on the
set very much. She works
in a small office and only
comes out at meal times.

SALLY
So where does she eat?

NATHAN
I'm glad that you asked.
At my favourite place on

the television set—the
canteen!

BILLY
Yeah, they have really
great food there! But
before we go and check
it out, there is one more
person to meet.

NATHAN
Who's that?

BILLY
Our safety co-ordinator,
Shey.

SALLY
She's going to be the most
important person on the
set.

BILLY
Shey is an extreme sport
expert. Her job is to make

sure that everything we do
is safe.

SALLY
Extreme sports can be
really dangerous if
they're not supervised
very carefully.

*SHEY walks onto the set
and stands beside Nathan,
Billy and Sally.*

SHEY
Congratulations on winning
the audition.

BILLY
I can't wait till we start
the extreme sports.

SHEY
They'll be heaps of fun.
Before we start, we must
have the right equipment.

And, of course, we must all know exactly what's involved in every sport.

BILLY
Today we've met most of the crew. Next episode we'll be whitewater rafting. Until then you've been watching *The Xtreme World of Billy Kool.*

DIRECTOR
Well that's a wrap. That wasn't too bad.

NATHAN
I think it's time we tried out the canteen.

BILLY
So do I.

SALLY
I hope everybody else has had something to eat. There won't be anything left after you've finished.

NATHAN
Is there a canteen on location?

FIRST ASSISTANT DIRECTOR
There is! And do you know the best thing about it?

NATHAN
What's that?

FIRST ASSISTANT DIRECTOR
It's free!

THE WRAP UP

It was awesome at the studio, except
the bit where they put make-up on
us. Nathan and I have made a pact
not to tell anyone. Sally said she's
going to tell *everyone*.

After Ally had edited the footage,
they screened the episode for us. It
was excellent.

They put in the footage of us
abseiling, and they showed some of
the other groups auditioning as well.
Two people had refused to go over

the edge. We were definitely the best.

Right at the end they showed footage of all the extreme sports we'd be doing. When I saw the skydiving footage, some butterflies crept into my stomach. One mistake and it could be splat, and I don't want that splat to be me. I must remember to pull the cord in the parachute.

If I had butterflies before … well I really had heaps after watching that. I'm glad Shey is going to be there.

Extreme Information

History

The term 'extreme sport' was first heard around 1995, when an American TV station was planning to televise Extreme Games—now called the X Games. But extreme sports have a long history.

Three factors contributed to the rise of extreme sports—the fitness revolution of the 1970s, the environmental movement of the 1980s and 90s, which created a renewed interest in the outdoors and wilderness areas, and advances in technology.

The death-defying sports seen on television have their origins in many everyday sports. For example, mountain biking grew out of cycling. Many extreme sports are even older. People have rock climbed throughout history. Whitewater rafting grew out of rafting and canoeing, which were early forms of transport.

Extreme sports are about danger, adrenaline, and taking the mind and body to the very edge.

Over time, extreme sports have become absorbed into the mainstream, though snowboarding is the only extreme sport to have become an Olympic sport.

Technological advances in television and film mean that these sports can now be seen from the comfort of most people's living rooms.

Glossary

Boom
The boom is a light-weight pole, like a long arm, that holds a microphone.

Call sheet
A form outlining the day's scenes, and the cast and equipment required for shooting.

Camera operator
The camera operator shoots the footage.

Clapperboard
The clapperboard helps the editor synchronise the images and sound.

Cutting room
The cutting room is where the editor decides which footage to include.

Director
The director tells the actors what to do

and plans the shots they want recorded.

Dolly

A dolly is a mobile platform that cameras
are mounted on for use in the studio.

Editor

The editor takes the footage into the
cutting room and splices the footage into
the television show.

First assistant director

The first assistant director is the director's
main assistant.

Gunshot microphone

If the actors aren't wired for sound, a
gunshot microphone is held above them
out of camera-shot to record sound.

Make-up artist

All actors have to wear a bit of make-up.
A make-up artist puts this on.

Producer

The producer plans the content of the television show.

Rehearse

To practise for the final performance.

Shoot

Another word meaning 'to film'.

Sound recordist

The sound recordist is in charge of capturing sound such as dialogue.

Studio lights

Studio lights are used when filming in a studio.

Video recording

Video recording is the process of recording on a video tape recorder. Television programs are recorded on video.

PHIL KETTLE

Phil Kettle lives in inner-city Melbourne, Australia. He has three children, Joel, Ryan and Shey. Originally from northern Victoria, Phil grew up on a vineyard. He played football and cricket and loved any sport where he could kick, hit or throw something.

These days, Phil likes to go to the Melbourne Cricket Ground on a winter afternoon and cheer on his favourite Australian Rules team, the Richmond Tigers. Phil hopes that one day he will be able to watch the Tigers win a grand final—'Even if that means I have to live till I'm 100.'

THE Xtreme WORLD OF BILLY KOOL

by Phil Kettle

Billy Kool books are available from most booksellers. For mail order information please call Rising Stars on 01933 443862 or visit www.risingstars-uk.com

First published in Great Britain in 2005 by
RISING STARS UK LTD.
76 Farnaby Road, Bromley, BR1 4BH

First published in Australia by Scholastic Australia in 2004.
Text copyright © Philip Kettle, 2004.

A Black Hills book, produced by black dog books

Designed by Blue Boat Design
Cover photo: Blue Boat Design

For more information visit our website at:
www.risingstars-uk.com

British Library Cataloguing in Publication Data

A CIP record for this book is available from the British Library

ISBN 1 905056 40 0

Printed by Bookmarque Ltd, Croydon, Surrey

If I win the contest I'll be doing some of the most awesome extreme sports in the world. I'll be a TV star. And my two best friends will get to come along for the ride. How cool would that be?